One Pair of Shoes

One Pair of Shoes

Poems and stories
by a remarkable woman

MOLLIE PEACE

1920 – 2007

ISBN 978-1-907203-39-8

Typesetting by Wordzworth Ltd
www.wordzworth.com

Cover design by Titanium Design Ltd
www.titaniumdesign.co.uk

Printed by Lightning Source UK
www.lightningsource.com

Cover photograph and editing by Nigel Peace

Published by Local Legend
www.local-legend.co.uk

For everyone

who ever wanted to be a writer

Contents

One Pair of Shoes

A lifetime with one pair of shoes.
If only.
I'll choose the shiny pair with buckles
so delightful in those childhood days
and hours of wonder
and naivety.

Could we but choose
when paths are steep and shoes worn thin
to wear the shiny pair
with buckles.

Alas,
we grow out of them.
Life becomes a long and weary walk
and shiny shoes with buckles
have no place
on its rough ways.

Is Daddy Home

The firelight flickers and the cat purrs on,
hot buttered crumpets in the hearth
wait there
as children sprawled with heads in
sticky hands
stare pensively through flames.

And each one asks
"Is Daddy home?"

The snow still falls,
we quietly wait,
the youngest ones impatient now
but know that crumpets,
soaked and hot,
are better far when footsteps and a creaking gate
tell Daddy's home.

Mollie was one of six children, living with their parents in a small cottage in a rural Oxfordshire village. They were poor and life was hard. But she never forgot the happy times of childhood, such as the simple joys of having new shoes or a family gathered by the fireside. These images stayed with her as counterpoint to the challenges of adult life.

Granny Time

Granny, can I come and sit beside you
while you tell me of the things-that-used-to-be?
Of course, my child, come over here
although I fear
you're much too old to sit upon my knee.
We'll have our supper as we talk,
pork roast, potatoes, garden greens
(a glass of parsnip wine for me).
Where shall I start - ?

But Granny –

Never interrupt, my child,
and by the way
you've too much on your plate.
In old Victoria's time a child had manners,
seen not heard,
taught patience,
had to wait.

But Granny –

What is it that you have to say
that cannot keep 'til night?
So hush, you talk too much
and spoil our appetite.
Children have to understand
unspoken words,

be seen not heard,
to mind their Ps and Qs,
or get a strict and searching look from those
not interested in their views.

But Granny –

My child, I'm happy that you came today
to ask what-used-to-be,
so listen
even though it seems
a most old-fashioned way.

But Granny –

There you go and interrupt again.
That anguished look must mean you are in pain.
What is it, child?

It's too late, Gran,
but funny too –
the caterpillar on your greens
is inside you.

Big City

My mother said Goodbye, Goodbye
meaning God be with you,
while my father shook my hand and told me
things that I already knew.

He braced his shoulders,
mother wept,
but I had kept my promise to myself
that when I came of age
I'd show the world.

Whitewash

Not many can claim that their greatest happiness started in a privvy up the garden path, a little whitewashed hut among the wildflower patch. Those walls were just too tempting for a six year old to ignore.

Her father was a master carpenter whose pencils were long and flat, especially the nub ends which were too short for workmen to use and therefore a delight for small children. The siblings would watch and wait for the day when Father's pencil became used up, constantly squabbling over such a simple thing, yet a treasure in a family too short of money for toys.

"Mine! My turn."

"You had the last one!"

When she had the nub end, imagination took over in the whitewashed hut among the flowers. At first a poem, cut short by "You've been up there long enough, my girl!" Though on her next visit, two lines had been added. Indoors, she looked quietly at her brothers and sisters, while Father's dark brown eyes twinkled. Eventually, Mother's patience with the word-splashed walls would run out – "If I ever find out who's doing this..." – and there'd be fresh whitewash to contemplate.

As the children grew, the others gave up their fight for the nub ends and her passion developed on stray scraps of paper taken off to the fields beyond the cottage, beside a running brook. Poetry. Composition. Miss Snubnose, form teacher, refused to believe they were the work of a village girl. Imagination retreated.

War clouds loomed, there was work to do, then marriage and children of her own and – ha! – their homework compositions, their imagination to encourage, the pictures of their mental worlds to draw. She started again, immersed in the daily joy of good words in scrap books. And with the children flown the nest, she was accepted by the local magazine. Happiness, and the gift passed down to grandchildren, using pens a little more substantial than a nub end.

Some years later she visited an elderly relative's cottage in the village and was surprised to find a privvy up the garden path. Even more surprising was the discovery that it had three seats. Given that, she would never even have started...

It almost seems incredible to us in the twenty-first century that within one lifetime conditions had been so primitive and children satisfied, even excited, by such simplicity and privation. It is a powerful lesson to us that what matters most in life are family and the ideas and determination of our minds, and that we must never forget the effort and gifts, hard fought, of those who have gone before us.

Conscience

Father was a great one for ambling. He always reckoned there was an art to it, if you ambled properly. It clears the mind, he'd say, and you get to see things other folk never see in a lifetime. Sunday mornings would find us children regularly ambling with him, to keep us out of Mother's way while she cooked the huge roast with Yorkshire pudding.

"See what I've found," he'd call out to us, and we'd rush back to stand looking in awe at the shining bright new penny nestling in the grass near his feet. Somehow my younger brother John was always first on the scene to claim this find and he fell for it every time. Of course, as we grew older and realised that brand new pennies don't just keep getting themselves lost, Father had to think up other discoveries. At least it taught us to keep our eyes open.

Father continued to amble throughout his lifetime, but as he grew older his wits weren't always so sharp.

The letter came flying over the fence just as he was busy turning up his coat collar and pulling down his cap against the high autumn wind. Being so occupied, he gave it as much notice as a ticket tossed carelessly from the upper deck of a bus. It wasn't until he was swinging his long legs over a stile that the sight got through to his brain and got a second glance. Balancing in mid-swing like a gymnast, he gave the matter some thought. It was a letter all right. No doubt whipped from the hand of some youngster sent out with it by his auntie; he'd be too afraid to go back and admit that he'd posted it in the teeth of the wind instead of the mouth of the letterbox. Father chuckled at his own joke and leaned over as the wind considerately blew the envelope right to his feet.

Strange, there was no address. But the envelope was open

and a letter plainly visible inside. Father turned the matter over in his mind for a few minutes – he always liked a bit of rumination – and decided that it was no business of his. He picked up the envelope and stuffed it in the pocket of his old leather jacket, then swung himself back over the stile to continue his usual route along Primrose Lane and across Jim Backer's dairy ground. He'd hand the letter in at the Post Office later.

His thoughts were interrupted by a shout to his left where he saw his old crony Fred Duckett bent over in apparent agony, trying to attract Father's attention, his wicker cadging basket by his side.

"Gi' us an 'and then, Will," he called out. "Me back's gorn agen."

Father ambled over, helped Fred to straighten up, and then bent down himself to admire the half-dozen large pink mushrooms in his basket. Of course, Fred was now obliged to share his discovery and the two men, all other responsibilities forgotten by the prospect of a good fry-up later, set about their serious work of filling the basket. They must have got a fresh half peck, though it took an hour inbetween their yarns and Fred's frequent coughing fits.

"Sounds rough," observed Will, with a talent for stating the obvious.

"Ar, that young Bones'll be comin' over later. Check me out, like."

"Well, 'least you'll have a fine supper inside you." Will nodded at the basket as they reached the fork to make their separate ways home.

"Nah, the missus's at 'er sister's fer the day. Gorn since seven. Not back 'til the ten-thirty bus. Her'll not likely want to cook then."

With all that ambling and ruminating in the wet grass, Father tarried too long and found himself that evening with a temperature, feeling drowsy and fair middlin', as he would say. Next morning Mother made him stay in bed until she'd made up the fire and aired the room, and he was dozing peacefully until woken by the sound of the front door and quiet voices from downstairs. Striving to collect his thoughts and clear his head, he lay quietly for a few minutes in the darkened room until, for some reason, his eyes were drawn to the chair at the end of the bed. Over the back of it was his old leather jacket and suddenly Father was wide awake, his conscience crying out. The letter! He'd completely forgotten about it.

His thumbs twiddled madly under the bedclothes nervously until finally he rose quietly and crept through the shadows to the bedroom door, a draught from the open window stirring his nightshirt. He could still barely hear the voices with the door at the foot of the stairs closed.

With almost paralytic fingers, he slipped the envelope and a box of matches from his jacket pockets before edging down the cold stone stairs and sitting halfway. Now he could make out Mother's soothing voice. When the other woman spoke, he recognised her as Fred's missus.

"The old fool'd never do as he was told. When I left yester-morn I gave 'im a letter. But 'e couldn't even do that. Now what am I going to do?"

Father clutched the collar of his nightshirt in panic, his grey hair bristling on the back of his neck as if ghosts were circling around him in the tiny stairwell. What had he done? Old Fred had been real rough yesterday, said the doctor was coming over later. But...? And now his missus was here and all upset. Icy fingers crept up Father's spine with the enormity of what he'd done. Finally he eased the letter from its envelope and struck a match. In the soft flickering light he read:

"Dear Milky, it be Fred's birthday. Please leave three extra pints, eggs and cream for the cake." It was signed Mrs Amy Duckett.

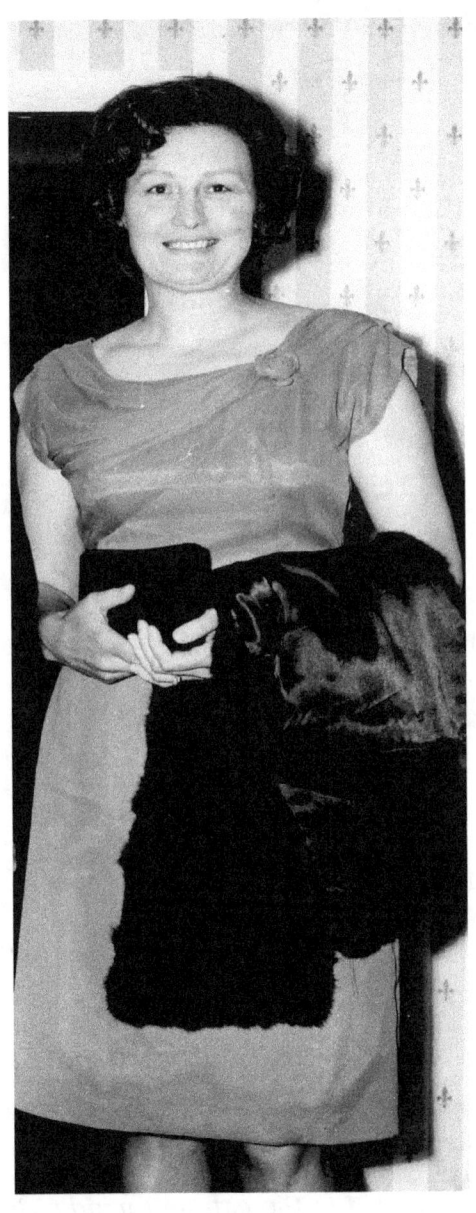

We Must Have Winter

Heavy,
thick,
the snow lies bathed in winter sun,
shadowed by trees
as bare as babes.
No life,
not one thing stirs to change the
stillness,
colour none,
no promise of a future.

But wait!
The scene has changed
and colour bright as Flanders poppies
weaves a timid pattern.

We needed just the robin
and he came
with life
and future yet untold.

Growing up in the English countryside, Mollie had a deep love for nature, closely observed, especially for birds and trees. This never left her, and when she moved to the city and middle-class suburban life its imagery lived on in her writing as metaphors for the seasons of human experience.

Night Song

He was black,
the setting sun behind him,
polished ebony.

His voice rose high and free,
full-throated happiness,
so I laughed with him
and our voices flew together over trees
that shook with merriment and
lifted branches high in pleasure
as the hills gave back their echo.

The wind bore it over seas,
high in the breasts of gulls
to other shores,
and there the brothers of my friend
would hear the song of freedom
as their sun rose.

Yesterday

There was a time when fields were free,
a place of peace for you to be
and sit until the sun went down
where troubles ceased,
and ne'er a frown to spoil the beauty of the hour.
And then the distant cuckoo call
on gentle breezes saying goodnight
to the trees that stand so tall.

Down by the stream
the creatures that by day are busy
in their own small ways
are now at rest and no doubt thinking of
another day,
while those that wake while we as mortals rest
begin to fly high on another quest.

But where is now the peace there was
that we as children never questioned?
Did we value not enough
the days of freedom offered by the fields?

We wished that peace and freedom for ourselves
while creatures
always knew and never questioned it.

Willow

She stands so proud in sun's caress,
coquettish laughter,
lifted petticoats
and dancing with her friend the breeze,
enjoying without thought the freedom
so denied to many others,
whispering her confidences
to the winged souls on her mother arms,
resting now and dreaming.

But come the storm
and dreams are tossed
into a wilderness and broken.

Yet she stays
and comes again the sun
and souls
to warm cold limbs
and ease her sickness.

New days dawn,
she stands so proud again,
a living, dancing dream.

Benjamin Versus the Young 'uns

Ben thought he was clever, though the rest of the village includ-
ing his wife Martha weren't so sure about that. But it went
against the grain for him to expend energy on a competition of all
things. Folk would wonder later how they had missed this,
things being what they are in a small place. Ben had lived all his
seventy-eight years in sleepy Closeford (pop. 359), a place that
had changed very little because the old 'uns liked it that way and
the young 'uns didn't care much. The city commuters who'd
moved in in recent years had their cars, while a good bus service
or a boyfriend's motorbike were all that was needed for the kids
to keep in touch with the social life of Burberry, the nearest
town.

But things changed the day the local council announced an
allotment competition for next springtime, with prizes for neatest
layout and best soil. Catalogues were hurriedly brought out from
beneath sofa cushions, cash boxes inspected and spades sharp-
ened.

The announcement was received with delight and over-
confidence by the old 'uns, who instantly decided that this was a
matter of pride and tradition versus naïve new-fangled science.
"They young 'uns ain't got patience, that they ain't," was the
verdict of the experience generation over their ale in the Five
Bells snug on a Friday night. Townies might have more money,
more strength, and 'modern ideas', but they were no match for a
lifetime of soil under the fingernails.

The days went by, spades flashing, some in rhythmic strokes
and others at a pace impossible to last. Ben worked steadily,
taking just the odd moment to shift his eyes warily across to the
new allotments where the young 'uns worked. A small voice
broke through his thoughts.

"My Dad says you old 'uns have no chance, my Dad says." Straightening up slowly and turning round, Ben saw the Weedon boy, pink, undersized and, as Ben would say, with a button missing.

"What were that, lad?" he growled. Recognising the tone, Bert shuffled nervously and inspected his shoes.

"My Dad says you haven't got a fair chance, that's all. Says it's not reasonable."

"'E does, does 'e, your Dad?" observed Ben, fixing the poor lad with an ancient stare. "Well, you tell your Dad 'e can look out. I'll give 'im reasonable. Now, git off my piece, young varmint." Bert Weedon got off.

But his remarks troubled Ben, who'd been thinking much the same himself five minutes before. Taking a good, but of course casual, look at the hive of activity beyond, the bags of top-grade manure and suspicious packets of chemicals, he muttered "The boy might 'ave a point" to himself. It was then that Benjamin came to his decision.

So it was that the rest of the company saw old Ben leave his piece, spade dragging along the ground with difficulty, and make his way very very slowly to the gates on a circuitous route. Along the paths he emitted several strange grunts and completed the picture by doubling up with what he hoped sounded like a terminal bout of coughing adjacent to the new pieces. He made sure they all saw him. Heads turned. The man of experience and gardening authority was leaving his allotment less than half-dug with hours of daylight left.

In the cottage, Martha muttered to herself, her hands dug deep into the washing up to her elbows in soap.

"Can't git on no how this morning," she muttered to no-one in particular, "copper fire black as yer 'at an' the old dog under me feet. Summat in th'air today. Good thing Ben's out o' the way on his allotment. Finish things if 'e were wanderin' about the place." She banged the washing into the clothes basket, balanced it on her hip and made for the back door just as it opened and Ben wandered in. She reeled and dropped the basket as he stood still, hopefully looking the picture of misery.

"Well, yer dinner ain't ready so you can jest git back to yer diggin'," she observed unsympathetically. "Whatever you thinking comin' 'ome this hour?" Having thus dismissed her husband, she picked up the washing and made her way into the garden. After a while she called back: "Ben, you there? Bring me some more pegs, behind the pantry door." No answer.

Not used to being ignored, Martha hurried in to find Ben slumped in his old wicker chair, eyes closed and breathing with apparent difficulty. She softened and touched his sleeve.

"Ben? You all right?"

"Ah."

"You do' look all right, Ben. Tekken cold, dare say. Would you like a cup o' cocoa?"

"Ah. I do feels cold, girl. Think I'll tek a brick and git me to bed," he mumbled.

"To bed, man?" Martha was shaken. "It ain't even dinner time."

"I'll git me to bed," he repeated, heaving himself up and walking slow as he could to the stair door. "Bring the cocoa, girl." The washing now forgotten, Martha made the drink and took it upstairs to find Ben already burrowed deep beneath the blankets.

"Never knew you tek on like this afore, Ben, never," she addressed the hump of bedclothes. "Bin ill, you 'ave, but never sudden like. 'Ere, drink this an' I'll go an' fetch our Alice."

Ben couldn't abide Martha's sister with her eagle eyes and withering glares. "Meddlin' woman," he'd say. She thought all troubles could be cured by strange tasting teas and home-made compresses that smelled disgusting. "Don't want 'er..." he called out, but Martha had already gone and he heard the gate click. "That's done it," he muttered to himself, and decided to try sleep. But he'd barely started counting sheep when the door opened again and he heard Alice's shrill voice declaring that men were all the same, all babies in her opinion who didn't deserve the time of day. He closed his eyes tight, opened his mouth and snored heavily.

"Disgusting!" said Alice, confirming her own opinions.

"Ben, I've brought our Alice," said Martha, shaking his shoulder gently. "She'll 'ave a look at you. She's 'ad training, you know, an' I do' want to bother that nice young doctor if it ain't necessary. Ben...?"

...thirty-four, thirty-five, thirty-six...

"'E do look peeky, though," observed Alice, her face peering so close to his he could feel her minty breath. "An' I dursn't tek 'is temperature with 'is mouth all lolled open like that lest 'e swallows it. Hmm, 'e do look peeky." Ben was so surprised by these kindly remarks that he lost count of the sheep and had to start again.

So the nice young doctor came after all and Ben could hear him talking to Martha downstairs. "Nothing serious, just a chill you understand. Send along for this medicine and keep him warm." Then he seemed to raise his voice and direct it towards the stairs. "Plenty of fruit drinks, nothing intoxicating of course. And no food 'til I see him again. I'm sure he'll be fit as a fiddle in a few days. Can't have him laid up, can we?" Darn, thought Ben.

The old 'uns were in near panic in the Five Bells snug come Friday night. Ben was their golden hope in the competition. What he didn't know about gardening could be written on a seed packet. Meanwhile, the young 'uns took the news calmly and had their own meeting in the saloon. As for Ben, he didn't like the way things were going at all. No food? No beer? And the medicine was of course horrible. Then there was the visit from old Tom who just kept shaking his head and saying that the young 'uns had nothing to stop them now. There was time later for the planting, but everyone knew the real secret was in the digging...

Two days later found Ben remarkably recovered and able, on doctor's orders, to take a gentle stroll in the winter sunshine. So he made his way to the allotments and found exactly what he'd known he would find. His piece was fully dug, neatly turned over and ready for planting.

Springtime came and brought renewed feverish activity in the allotments. With energy that surprised more than a few, Ben worked right through to the end of planting.

But when the day of the judging came, a heavy hailstorm flattened almost everything, young plants being no match for the storm's temper. The allotments were under water for a week.

Nowadays, the young 'uns are happy to ask Ben for advice on their gardens. But he doesn't sleep so well now, and keeps losing count of the sheep.

Unwelcome Visitors

Getting rid of unwelcome visitors can be a tricky problem, unless you've been fortunate enough to have been schooled in the wiles of Father. Always possessive of his home and family, and never caring for having "odd folks" around the place, in time he got it down to a fine art and never once did he lose a friend in the doing. Maybe it was his big, honest, brown eyes that fooled people, but they never seemed to realise they'd been got rid of.

The favourite ruse when he felt particularly unsociable was to hint at some undefined illness and embark on a good scratching session. He would start in one spot with a gentle rub and then work up to a hefty continual scratch until before long the visitor would become convinced that he'd caught something and start scratching in sympathy, then making a hasty retreat. The only one this didn't work on was Mother's sister Alice whom he could never abide. The dear annoying soul would advise senna pods for any ailment from the obvious to the ridiculous, and having had some sort of 'training' was not about to be put off by a bit of an itch.

Mother, too, picked up some of his skills over the years. A far more sociable person at heart, she did it just to keep the peace although she probably secretly enjoyed the game too. She would answer the door wearing her shopping hat. If the visitor was unwelcome it would be "Oh dear, and we was just going out"; alternatively it was "Now then, you're lucky to catch us, we'm just got back."

Next to family, the love of Father's life was horses and what he didn't know about horses you wouldn't care about. During the Depression years he was driven from his master trade to hiring a horse and cart and setting up a travelling fish and greengrocery round. He cared greatly for the old cob, rubbing her down at the end of the day, talking gently and teasing her with sugar lumps.

And as a child I would be out waiting for them on their return from the round to help out in any way I could. Fetching and carrying were all right with me. When "Whoa" sounded at the gate I'd run down the driveway to greet them and get a ride atop the old cob up the last few yards.

Our annoying neighbour Tom would often be out there too, hanging over the fence and offering advice on the care of old horses.

"How do, Will. She behave 'erself today, then? You do' want to tek no nonsense. What I suggest is…"

Father came up with a string of ways to get rid of him and pretty soon Betsy learned to join in. Father would begin the rub down after unharnessing her and I'd swear the two of them shared a wink. The old cob was tired after a good day's work and looking forward to some peace and quiet, so just as Father slapped her backside she obliged with a final contribution to the day, right at Tom's feet. Father blandly turned to the man and said "Fetch us a bit of lavvy paper, then." Only when Tom returned after a few minutes with a small pile of cut newspapers did he realise he'd been taken in, and beat a retreat. Betsy got an extra sugar lump, a slap on the rear and a "Thanks, girl."

Unfortunately, though, the old cob developed an inconvenient association of ideas and began to contribute indiscriminately. It got Father into trouble more than once. Sometimes he would have a customer keep him talking too long or haggling over some quite unimportant matter relating to his purchase, so a slap on the horse's rump was a signal for her to move on. But Betsy came to associate this with an offering on her part and a sugar lump in reward, and all too often the customer would have to be placated with an extra apple or a bit over the pound of cod's roe. On the other hand, their roses did well.

There was one occasion when Father was completely defeated by unwelcome attention, a Saturday evening when he was having his weekly bath. Being over six feet tall, he sat with knees high in the tin bath in front of the range and settled down to a good soaping. Normally the children would by now be in bed or well out of the way and that went for the old family dog too. But she had hid herself under the dining table and now became unusually inquisitive. Circling round the back of the bath, she began to lick the soap from Father's back and, rather liking the taste, she then ambled round to the side and began to drink the water, bringing up an alarming shout of objection.

"You little varmint, git out on it!" Father flicked the dog with his towel but her daily yeast tablets must have given her too much energy and she assumed this was a new game. Without ado Father stepped from the bath and the chase began, to cries of "You little bugger!" and "Dratted animal!"

The commotion brought Mother running from the scullery. She came to a halt with hands on hips and mouth wide in amazement, not sure whether to laugh or be angry, as she watched Father hop out of the bath as the dog hopped in. It was like watching sheep over a stile, in and out, in and out they went, the old spaniel loving every splash of the water. When Father abandoned the towel it was Mother's turn to join in, with Father now trying to avoid the dog and Mother bringing up the rear trying to get the towel round his naked wet waist.

The pantomime eventually ended with the dog cornered, towelled down and packed off to her kennel, and a few choice words exchanged between my parents. But they never noticed the other unwelcome visitor hiding in the shadows under the big dining table.

This Work Is Yours

Weave your piece of tapestry
then take your cloth and hold it gently.
Colours must be bold.
They must be yours,
no matter what the world decides.

So will you weave it golden
for the freedom of the sun,
or will you choose dark colour
for the night?
Yours is the only choice.

Be they black or brown or murky grey
or big, bold, beautiful and bright,
no matter how the tapestry is woven
it's no use blaming others for mistakes.

Here is my piece of tapestry,
my Lord.
I'll do my best.

The Second World War broke out with Mollie still in her teens. She worked as an ambulance driver and then a telephonist, and married Ron, an army Captain. Within just a very few years she moved from close-knit family and simple country life to independence, falling in love, the horror of conflict and the loss of loved ones, including a child. For her generation, the pain of these experiences lived on.

You Must Decide

Stand beneath the cherry tree
and lift your eyes
just for a moment
for that's all the world may give you.

This moment rare,
a moment to decide that life is full
or void,
it lasts or like pink blossom falls
when winds of fate blow
cold indifference.

Is there a haze of pink beyond
or do green leaves make sturdy arms
to hold you from your yesterdays?
You must decide.

A War

There must have been a war
or something
since the last time we embraced.
Your loving arms are not there
any more.
Was it a war of stress within
or hate?
I only know I cannot wait.
Without your loving arms,
life will go on
but there begins my war.
There's no safe place for me to go,
where can I hide
when it is always 'no'.
Without your arms I shall soon fall
in the fight
so show me that there never was
a war.

Quiet Star

There was a time when we would gaze together at the stars
and say
are they so very far away?
And as we looked there always seemed to be
one special star
that shone for you and me.
That star shone brightly through the years
and guided us together
through our many hopes and fears.

But then one evening I looked high,
the star dimmed gently
and I heard you sigh.

And over fields came dawn's soft murmur
with a new star born
as you, my dear beloved, join the sky,
a myriad of love that shines only for me.

And so I sleep relaxed in love.
And until we meet again I shall forever see
the beauty of the starry night,
the glory of my own quiet star
shining for me.

Let It Be Now

If I must die, let it be now.
Now,
while quiet is here and war has ceased,
now,
while snow is virgin and the day is mine.
Let it be now.
Now,
while fires glow warm and faces therein
send their love
for with tomorrow's ash
I cannot live.
If I must die, let me know
peace,
let my heart beat in unison with yours.
So take my hand and let it please be
now,
in sunshine quiet on snow.

Happy Birthday To My Child

Soft spring breezes
to bring warm anticipation.

Summer sun
a mantle to the world's indifference.

Autumn colours
to bring contentment to the heart.

And winter
for its jewelled landscapes
and its promise
of tomorrow.

The Fifties were hard times for many. But people were resilient and full of hope for the future. The family settled to suburban city life, a world away from everything that Mollie had grown up with. Her writing now expressed the joys and insecurities of those days.

Flashback

She dreams her dreams
and schemes,
she's up, she's down
and does the town.

Just like I did.
My daughter.

Neglects her pets,
jellies won't set,
hair up, hair down,
black shoes with brown.

Just like I did.
My daughter.

She loves the boys but
keeps her toys,
nose up, nose down,
wears a teenage crown.

Just like I did.
My daughter.

A Promise

The garden sleeps
no more to hear the happy shouts of children,
tender grass no more to feel the stamping of their feet,
daisies long since withered by persistent plucking fingers
and even birds have stilled their songs.

But later on when God has rested
nature will awake refreshed
and ready to spill gaiety from her bosom
and fill my heart again with that eternal spring.

MOLLIE PEACE
1920 - 2007

Bored On A Board

I refused to be plastered – "No thanks, not this time" - and was somewhat startled when the young orthopaedic feller didn't even lift his eyes from the notes he was making. He was very nice, though, and obviously trying not to smile at my light-heartedness toward the situation. Well, I had a few years on him so that entitled me to have a little go. Especially as he was private. The trouble was a thin-as-a-wafer disc that caused me to hop from one foot to the other in continuous pain. You know how it is, you keep thinking it will go away at least until after the holidays and Christmas is behind you.

"Well," he said, thumbs and forefingers pinching the end of his nose, "it's two weeks in bed then." Just as I was beginning to feel enthusiastic at the thought of a fortnight away from the kitchen and the chores, his nose reacted violently to the stabbing fingers and he spluttered loudly, "Flat! Flat, I say. None of your sitting up. Flat. Except for the loo."

I didn't think it quite nice for an expensive orthopaedic feller to use such language, and he clearly caught my expression. Well, they aren't specialists for nothing.

"Toilet," he corrected himself, rustling my notes and adding, as if he considered all women idiots, "So cut down the fluids."

I floated out of the door on an air of blissful suffering at the thought of two whole weeks rest. Dead easy. The rest of the day was spent stocking up the fridge, then I retired to bed with a new lilac shortie I'd been looking forward to wearing ever since I'd bought it for myself last birthday.

The first two days were delightful, listening to the radio and lapping up the family's attention while they, I learned later, were lapping up a whole week's provisions. The third day I spent fascinated by learning several new ways of twiddling my thumbs and the fourth day I had to change the shortie because counting its buttons was driving me potty. By the end of the first week I'd cut out all the recipes from three years of saved magazines and become completely cross-eyed looking down my nose trying to write letters. The Sleeping Princess dream was fading. Yes, Prince Charming came to visit all right – holding up a dripping Finnan Haddock and asking what went wrong and why had the spinach turned his face country green. I had to wait a long time for my tea that day.

Then there was the puddle on the linoleum in the toilet. I suspect it was the small son of a visiting friend. Of course, I slipped on it which only made matters worse and for some reason Prince Charming got rather angry. But I got my own back, making a proper nuisance of myself with the little bell he'd provided for me to call for attention, thoroughly finishing off the bridge game going on downstairs.

From the eighth to the thirteenth day I tried, not too successfully, to entertain myself. First I picked on the spiders, two very small and perfectly innocent things probably having great fun together until my long-handled feather brush approached. Then I borrowed one of my young son's favourite pastimes and strew the room with paper pellets catapulted from a large and thick elastic band carelessly left within my reach. When I tired of that I decided that a trial run of some new eye make-up could be fun. I invite you to lie flat on your back and attempt a series of colour programmes to see what happens. Actually I was very much enjoying myself until I dropped the top set of false eyelashes into my open mouth. Panicking at the thought of surgery to cut open my stomach, I managed with difficulty to roll over onto one side and cough, projecting the offending thing onto the padded headboard where it stuck, leering at me for the rest of the day. Entertainment over.

To be fair, word of my boredom spread through the suburban jungle and several friends came and went, warily treading a path in the carpet around my bed. Unfortunately, Janice did sit down rather heavily on the cushion under which I'd cunningly hidden Mary's offering of a macaroni cheese. She should have known better, since I hate it. I only realised later that it had been meant for the family's dinner.

With one day to go I settled back in great anticipation of a good night's sleep before the morning brought the great lie-in to a thankful close. But Prince Charming had left the window open. With the morning also came a violent ear infection and high temperature. And another week in bed.

Bread Sauce

Women's intuition is seldom taken any notice of. Nevertheless, I did have that feeling as I reluctantly withdrew feet from warm bed and into cold slippers. I don't like Mondays anyway, so this kind of intuition certainly didn't help on that particular Monday morning.

Over the years I'd managed to train the family quite well, starting the week in a leisurely way, early and with a good breakfast. But there was something in the air today. Thinking back, though, it was all my husband's fault really. I mean, what sensible man puts down his knife and fork, wipes his mouth, and announces almost as an afterthought at eight-thirty that he's bringing his boss and his wife home for dinner that same evening? Then adds "And don't forget the bread sauce, darling."

You just knew that disaster would strike after such a statement. So I made myself an extra pot of tea putting such mundane things as bosses and bread sauce firmly to the back of my mind, fighting against them. Or maybe, as Mother would say, just "being okkard". As my fingers curled around the third cup of tea I remembered that small china pig standing on the mantelpiece at home when I was a child. It looked like any ordinary pig, but on the backside was printed "I won't be druv" and that's just how I was feeling. Bread sauce. It had to be home-made too of course. On a Monday. And I'd only recently come out of hospital with orders to have a quiet time. The teapot empty, I went upstairs to run my bath.

The first intimation of something wrong came as I returned to the kitchen. An unnatural quiet had descended upon the house and an intensely alert look on our small Sheltie's face stopped me in my tracks. She began to whine. I knew it. Intuition. You may laugh, but there was something wrong.

It was all too quiet. That is, until a persistent banging on the front door startled me into action. I was used to a more melodious bell. Half-way down the hallway and the telephone shrilled at me exactly as the back door opened with a crash and our neighbour called out "Oh dear!" throwing me into total confusion. We'd only been in the house a few weeks and it hadn't occurred to me that neighbours could take the liberty of bursting in.

With the banging and the shrilling and the shouting, I didn't know which way to turn. The telephone stopped, then shrilled again, another neighbour appeared from nowhere, and when I opened the door there was the screeching of brakes, raised voices, the clattering of equipment and running feet. All this frantic activity was now centred around our house, and apparently a major affair whatever it was. Through the haze, I do remember that. And I also remembered that I never did like Monday mornings.

Stunned by the suddenness of it all, I realised that any plans for the day were obviously now ruined. It seemed like an emergency to be faced, and I was quite unprepared for the discomfort of a main fuse blowing on an all-electric estate.

As the long morning slowly turned into afternoon it was becoming obvious to everyone that this was Something Big. Great specialists at famous hospitals perform long and wonderful operations daily and, in its own way, this was exactly what was happening on our doorstep. There were seven senior engineers with all their assistants keeping up a steady supply of sophisticated equipment, and a steady supply of steaming coffee passing from hand to hand too. Brows were wiped and consultations made. Students appeared too, invited to learn, peering into the already gaping incision. Some were observed to swallow hard and turn away, while others attempted half-hearted conversation and one was even heard to laugh. Anxiety takes people in different ways.

By three o'clock it was obvious to all present that this thing was Too Big for them. Better call in the real specialists. Four o'clock found the seven engineers joined by five more. After much head shaking, raised voices and a definite sense that all was not well, a decision was reached. A longer and deeper incision had to be made.

Four-thirty and they seemed forced to submit to failure. This looked terminal. Instruments were set down, a hurried conference called in the middle of the road and more flasks of coffee opened and distributed. Yet there can be inspiration in a hot drink. Suddenly an assistant who until now had taken no part in the proceedings started a whispered conversation, accompanied by several gesticulations, with one of the engineers while the others stood apart in silent groups guessing at what might be being said.

And then enlightenment broke through the strain and with smiles all round the operation was resumed with a new boldness. The old incision closed, they all moved left and cut again. Five-thirty. Success! The road was stitched up and tidied up and the whole terrible business over and done. One could only hope that the young assistant would receive his recognition and promotion.

So they all went home bathed in success. But not for me. Yes, intuition had been validated and I had survived the operation; but too late, and there was no chance of bread sauce.

Sunset

The day rose with the sun
red and silent
and a breeze spoke gently to me
as I touched a petal in its fall
still beautiful in its maturity.
A fox slunk past, brush drooping,
shifty ears laid back.
A giant sunflower nodded to the sun
as swallows twittered, blackbird carolled,
and the friendly willows waved the day begin
small river murmurs washing at their thin roots.

But now night shadows lengthen
and already swifts are high over the valley
as I try to stay the day.
The river hurries on.
And all too soon high stars of summer
shine through branches,
gleam on water
and, eager for their rest,
swifts home
and swallows like a great sigh rise to heaven.

An old oak tree stands firm without emotion
and shadows are now taller than the trees.
Still joyous,
blackbird sings his prayers.
The day is gone.
And as the sun also kneels down to pray
I'm drowsed
and I find peace.

MOLLIE PEACE
1920 - 2007

The Rose

Who will cull the rose
now the bloom has faded,
now that winter shows her hardened face?
Who will cup the flower now
in lover's hands
and say this once was my love?

No matter how much summer sun has warmed it
and the earth helped roots to gently grow,
the winter has to follow
and the rose must lose its bloom.

Life is short
so
who will cull the rose?

As time passed and the family grew up, troubles also began to grow in Mollie's mind. Ron had been scarred by his experiences and was also having to work long and difficult hours. Marriage became strained, though love survived. Mollie began to feel lonely, sometimes distant from her roots, but holding fast to the symbolism of nature in her writing.

Transition

Sometimes
a meandering path along a hillside,
gradual, unexciting,
a valley reached without effort
and no awareness
of the journey.
Sometimes
the rise and fall as of a frightened stallion,
sky and earth meeting,
changing levels,
limbs convulsed in fear
and no hand to steady them.
Sometimes
it's a roller coaster,
sharply rising, falling, tension slowing
then the calmness shattered once again
with an abrupt fall.
Falling.
Falling.
Sometimes
back on solid ground,
the clouds dispelled,
fruit of maturity,
the sunshine of purposeful living and
accomplishment.
There's thankfulness,
the wonder of transition.

Ours To Share

There are many gentle things in life
but none more gentle than the dawn,
before the day of noise and strife
as another day for us is born.

As on a bed of pain we lay
we thank God for another day.
The smallest bird is a promise there,
the day is ours and ours to share.
Perhaps we'll laugh, perhaps we'll mourn,
but now there's peace
in gentle dawn.

Mollie suffered considerable illness and pain yet, as the above writing shows, she never lost her optimism. Even when her beloved father died, she wanted to remember the laughter.

The Time Of The Pill

The day came when Father was ill. He was so seldom this way that it stayed with us for years to come. The greatest joy in life was his pipe, new every Christmas but decidedly antisocial by November. We were so used to the daily evening scene of him relaxing from a long day's work in his old wicker chair, the smoke of the pipe and the intermittent grunts that seemed to be a necessary part of the procedure for him, that we failed to notice when the grunts became more frequent. It was only when the family dog began to join in with him that we realised something was amiss.

He had always hated doctors. There was nothing personal about it and he was always good-tempered.

"A cup of cocoa and a good day to you, doctor."

But come the time when they needed to do something to him, it was quite another thing. To avoid the moment, his ways were wily and devious. Mother would make the drinks and place a plate of biscuits in the middle of the table, and with elbows in all the wrong places they would sit to have the customary chat (this was of course before the days of National Health, when doctors actually had time to chat) before getting round to the ailment. The family doctor, knowing Father's attitudes, would play along patiently before gently swinging the conversation round to "Well, what's the trouble then?"

But Father was ready. For several minutes already he would have been giving swift glances towards the stairway doors so it wouldn't be long before everyone else, being only human, would be unable to resist a glance there too.

"Did you hear that?" asked Father. The kindly doctor would of course turn to have a look, only to find in the few seconds before he turned back that Father had disappeared and with him most of the biscuits. Now, the old cottage had two staircases so the imagination doesn't need to work overtime. The doctor would make a dash for one set with Mother hot on his heels – strangely, they never did split up and take one each – only to find when they came back down that Father was sitting calmly at the table with an empty plate in front of him. Having had his fun, he might be ready to talk.

In the summertime it was a different story.

There were half a dozen wood sheds in a row, one for each cottage. Each one had a different door of course, but they shared the same roof space so that, if one had a mind to, one could enter one's own shed, lock it from the inside and then climb over dividing walls until emerging from an entirely different door. We seldom won on those occasions. One nice doctor we had knew the routine and would soon be out of the back door and along the path, the old dog puffing along at his heels, banging and pleading outside our shed. Then with stethoscope swinging he would pant up and down the row, convinced he had caught up, but somehow never noticing Father standing at the far end and grinning all over his weather-beaten face.

"Howdy-do," he'd say calmly, as if just arriving home from work.

That one time when he really was quite ill and in bed, even he knew that there was little chance of a chase beforehand. The doctor duly came and to our dismay a trip to the hospital, more than five miles away, seemed necessary. Waiting for the ambulance, Mother assumed that even Father couldn't get up to mischief now so she made him his cocoa and left him to snooze. She should have known better. It was no mean feat to get a stretcher up those curved stone staircases and the orderlies were not best pleased to find the patient missing. The hunt was on.

After ten minutes everyone was pretty fed up and prepared to call it a day. But Mother placated them with the offer of a hot drink and the promise of her special bread pudding. She made for the larder door and there he was, wiping his mouth on the back of his brawny arm, the dish empty.

Mind you, after he'd had his fun Father usually gave in quiet-
ly and was good company, so the journey to the hospital was
quite enjoyable. And for the first day or so he was a popular
patient, cooperative enough, never smoking his pipe except at
given times and endearing himself to the young nurses who
thought it a great giggle when he insisted on wearing his cap to
go to the toilet. Habits die hard and a lifetime of visits up the
garden path at any time of day or night called for a cap.

The doctor was also relieved to hear that no persons were
missing from the men's ward, but the peace was to be short-
lived. Father might not have absconded, but the trouble started
right enough when it was decided to treat him medically rather
than by surgery. Pills were the trouble. One small one, four times
a day, doesn't seem much to ask. But Father would only ever
take a pill when he decided to.

People pay several pounds to witness a pantomime half as good
as the one now enacted in Men's Medical. "And just one for you, my
love," smiled the small, sandy-haired nurse approaching Father's
bedside, offering a really very small pill from a spoon and reasona-
bly expecting his mouth to open as she tipped it up. It went down
the front of his nightshirt. He giggled, but kept his mouth shut. The
poor embarrassed nurse was covered in confusion, but orders are
orders and she had to get rid of that pill and in the right direction.
Cajoling didn't work so in desperation two large stalwart orderlies
were called in to lift him bodily and retrieve the pill.

The nursing staff next embarked on a series of crafty moves but
all to no avail. The ward was shaken from its slumbers by the
hilarious antics around bed five. It wasn't that Father was refusing
to communicate, but every question they tried could be answered
by a nod or shake of the head or a facial grimace. Smart Alec called
out that the only hope they had was to use a pea-shooter.

The end came when the Ward Sister decided to telephone the
next-of-kin (since 'phoning the family doctor would be to admit
defeat). It happened to fall to me.

"How can I give your father the pill?"

It seemed an odd suggestion at first, since Father was well into his seventies, had sired six children and had slept in his own bed for several years. And I didn't even know there was a pill for men. Realising how silly the thought was provided the answer.

"Just make him laugh!"

This turned out to be successful, but having learned the trick Father was ready for them when the next pill came round. So it wasn't surprising that a decision was soon made to discharge him back home. There, he was happy enough to stay in bed with a good supply of bread pudding. But Mother hadn't been married to him for more than fifty years without learning a thing or two. All sorts of things can be mixed into a pudding along with the fruit and suet.

Night

She walks so gently beside me,
there is no need for voice,
she knows my sorrows
and my joys,
she knows that I don't always have a choice.

Sometimes she'll take my hand
and give to me the peace I seek,
then with a smile
before she leaves
she'll make me understand
that while the night brings peace for all
by night or day
it has to come from me.

Without Sleep

Soft as a mother's touch
on fevered brow,
in silence falls the snow.
And trees already heavy with their burden
bow to the darkness.

The middle of the night and yet
no company for me
except the silence of my room.

The old dog in her bed
disturbed by dreams.

A dim lamp throwing shadows of the things
I want to see.

A clock somewhere
reminds me of tomorrow.

The snow falls straight,
the silence grows,
no sleep I know,
and if in heaven God is sleepless too
then burdened like the trees
I bow.

Ronnie

There was just a lantern held high by a Staff Nurse. The war was on and no lighting was allowed. The clock showed almost 3 a.m. when you gave a lusty cry.

"A boy. You have a baby boy." Sister peered into my face.

"He cried. I heard him cry," I said.

"Yes, but you mustn't expect him to live. He's much too premature."

"I don't expect anything now."

But I was devastated. It had been only a month before when, on sick leave from war work, the family GP had told me happily:

"You're pregnant, my dear. Five months."

Now I looked at you.

"Your Daddy will never see you. He's fighting in France."

They bundled you into a shawl, tidied you up and took you away. I was not allowed to hold you. No bonding. They baptised you with your father's name and I didn't see you again. Well-meaning friends said "You're young. You'll have other children."

And now much, much later I have been on a wonderful journey. I have seen you grown up in the spirit world and knew that you were there with me. You took my hand and said "I'm here, Mother, and I'll help you." I couldn't have taken that journey without your help.

Seasons Of The Sun

In spring
I loved my mother's arms and gentle voice,
the clock that chimed,
the padding of the old dog's feet,
the purring of the cat snatched from my cradle.
And then there was the sun to warm bare limbs
and stars that twinkled in my father's eyes.

In summer
I loved my lover's arms and gentle voice,
the warm, brown earth,
the chimes of love's awakening
sweet sounds of hearts in unison.
And then there was the sun to warm bare limbs
and stars that twinkled in a lover's eyes.

In autumn
I loved my children's arms and gentle voices,
the padding of small feet
and comforting merry-go-round
of happy sounds.
And still there was the sun to warm bare limbs
and stars that twinkled in a mother's eyes.

In winter
I loved but alone.
In dreams the quiet voices,
fluttering now of blackbird wing
and comfort of the blackness
of the night.
Did I forget the sun that warms tired limbs
and stars that twinkle in my Father's sky

MOLLIE PEACE
1920 - 2007

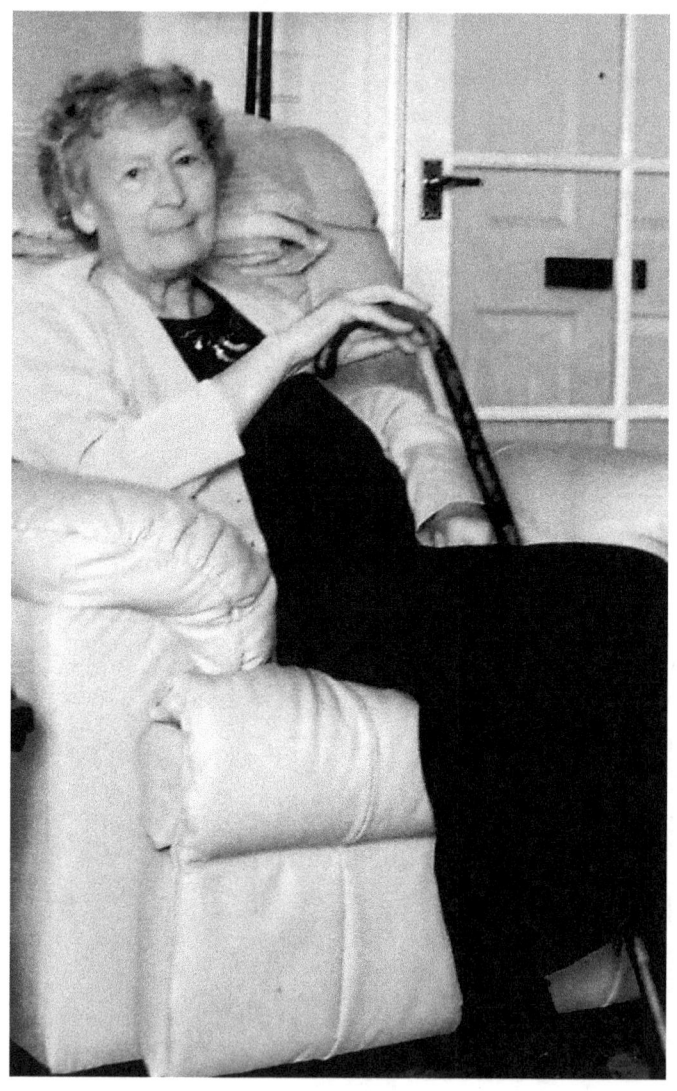